This book is for

_____

Conversations
on the
ARK

Written by Michelle Medlock Adams

Illustrated by Lucy Corvino

ideals children's books™
Nashville, Tennessee

ISBN 0-8249-5440-8

Published by Ideals Children's Books
An imprint of Ideals Publications
A division of Guideposts
535 Metroplex Drive, Suite 250
Nashville, Tennessee 37211
www.idealsbooks.com

Color separations by Precision Color Graphics, Franklin, Wisconsin

Printed and bound in Mexico by RR Donnelley.

Library of Congress Cataloging-in-Publication Data on File

10 9 8 7 6 5 4 3 2 1

For my sister, Martie.
Thanks for always believing in me.
Your little sis, Michelle.

And of every living thing of all flesh,
two of every sort shalt thou bring
into the ark. —Genesis 6:19

"What's going on?" the camel asked.
"Why are we on this ark?"
"I'm not sure," said the elephant.
"Let's ask the male aardvark."

The aardvark munched on several ants,
And then gave this reply:
"My mate and I just climbed aboard.
We're really not sure why."

Just then a chimpanzee swung by,
And he had this to say:
"According to the mockingbird,
It's gonna rain today."

"Oh, really," said the crocodile.
"It's never rained before!"
"That's true," the mockingbird replied.
"But we've got rain in store!"

"So, what is rain?" the boy bat asked.

"Does anybody know?"

"I think it's like a bunch of dew,"
Replied the female crow.

"A lot of dew sounds good to me,"
Chimed in the big bullfrog.
"Hey, Froggie's right. Rain might be fun!"
Replied the prairie dog.

The sky began to grow quite dark.

The rain would soon be there.

So Noah wandered through the boat

And counted every pair.

"Where are the snakes?" Noah called out.

"I haven't seen those two."

And then he felt them slithering

Across his sandal shoe.

"Oh, there you are," Noah exclaimed.
"I thought you were on board.
Well, that makes two of every kind.
We're ready, thank the Lord."

With that, the rain began to fall.
Then it began to pour.
When everyone was safe inside,
The Lord God shut the door.

"I think we're in for quite a ride,"
The alligator said.
The pig chimed in, "So where's the food?
I'm needing to be fed!"

"I hope we're not here very long,"
Complained the billy goat.
"I'm worried," said the antelope.
"You think this ark will float?"

"We'll know that answer very soon,"
Replied the big, brown cow.
"I never did learn how to swim.
I sure wish I knew how!"

And so the hours turned to days,
Each day just like the first.
"I'm tired of rain!" said Mr. Mole.
"This really is the worst!"

"Oh, stop complaining, Mr. Mole,"
Scolded a grizzly bear.
"Be thankful that you're here, inside,
Not drowning way out there!"

"Let's all just make the best of it,"
Declared the porcupine.
"I think this Noah guy's all right.
It all will turn out fine."

"I guess you're right," the mole replied.
"I'm just so tired of rain.
But that does not give me the right
To gripe, mope, and complain."

"I think the porcupine's on track,"
The lion blurted out.
"Just think, we're all getting along.
That's strange, without a doubt.

"Not even once," the lion said,
"Have I had the desire
To munch on you. It's really true.
This lion's not a liar!"

"Okay, let's change the subject now,"
Exclaimed the chickadee.
"I need to know what you guys think—
You think we will be free?"

The animals were at a loss.
Nobody said a word.
They all turned to the wise, old owl,
"Do you know, wise, old bird?"

The owl looked all around the ark,
And then had this to say:
"God's in control. We've all been spared.
We will be free someday."

A peaceful still came over them.
No growl. No squeal. No bark.
Each animal felt quite content
To be inside the ark.

Drip, drop. Drip, drop. The rain kept on
For forty days and nights.
And still the animals behaved—
No bickering or bites.

Then, suddenly, the raindrops stopped.

"Hooray! Hooray!" quacked Duck.

"Pipe down. I've got some real big news!"

Announced the brawny buck.

"That Noah guy sent out a dove
Who came back with a twig!"
"That means there's land nearby the ark!"
Rejoiced the female pig.

Then both giraffes stretched out their necks
To take a peek outside.
"Well, glory be!" the female said.
"We're through with this boat ride!

"There's lots and lots of land out there.
We're heading for the shore!"
Then Noah parked the big, old boat
And opened up the door.

"We're here! We're here!" the boy bat cheered.
"C'mon, let's check it out!"
"God saved us all," said Billy Goat.
"I never had a doubt."

The animals rushed off the ark,
And Noah said, "Good-bye."
Then God made something beautiful . . .

A rainbow in the sky.